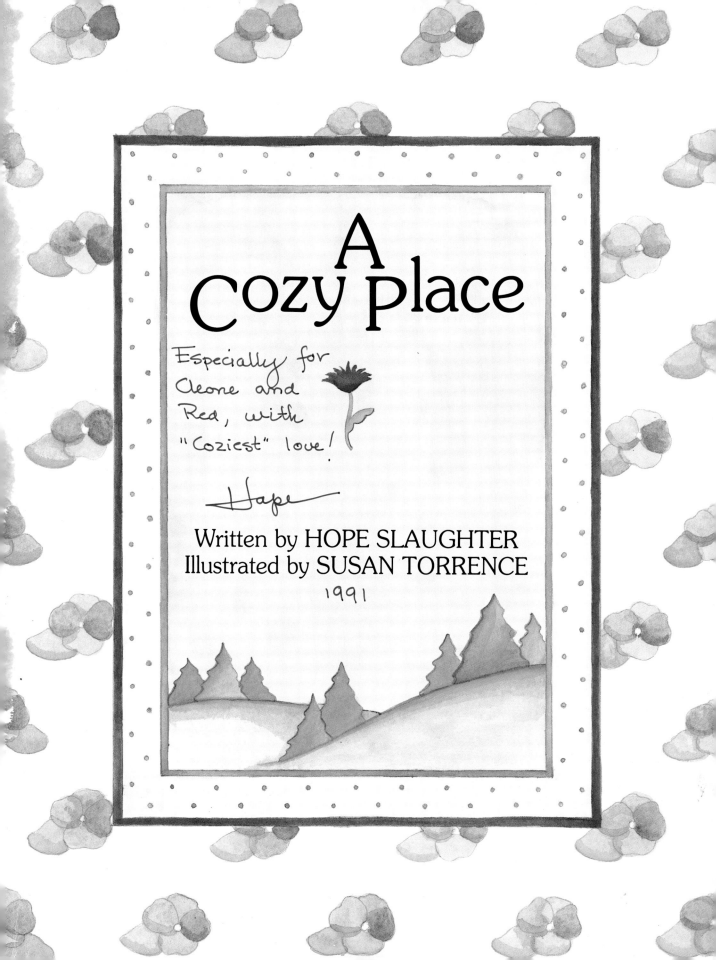

A Cozy place

Especially for
Cleone and
Red, with
"Coziest" love!

Hope

Written by HOPE SLAUGHTER
Illustrated by SUSAN TORRENCE

1991

Library of Congress Cataloging in Publication Data

Slaughter, Hope, 1940-
    A Cozy Place / by Hope Slaughter : Illustrated by Susan Torrence.
       p.   cm.
    Summary : Friends who enjoy creating "cozy places" discover that
places are only cozy when they are shared.
       ISBN 0-931093-13-9 : $15.95
       [l. Friendship--Fiction.]   I. Torrence, Susan, ill.   II. Title.
    PZ7.S63115Co   1990
    [E] - - dc20   90-49715
                                                           CIP
                                                           AC

Red Hen Press
P. O. Box 419
Summerland, CA 93067

Copies of this book may also be orderd directly from the
publisher: RED HEN PRESS, P.O. Box 419, Summerland, CA 93067
            $15.95 (Please include $1.00 for postage and handling)

To my wonderful parents, who have always made a cozy place for me. ---H.S.

To my sisters, Marcia and Nancy, who shared many cozy places with me when we were young. --- S.T.

My best friend Roberta and I never argue.

Except for yesterday.

I said our coziest place was under the card table when we put a blanket over it that touched the floor.

Roberta said our coziest place was
behind her sofa when we piled pillows
at one end until it was almost dark.

Then I said it was cozier when we made a snow house on the back hill last winter and filled it with piles of soft pine needles.

Roberta said that wasn't nearly as cozy
as the tent we made under the clothesline with
the old sheet.

"Well," I said, "what about the house we made with the box my mother's new washing machine came in? We even had curtains."

Roberta shook her head. "We couldn't even stand up in there!" she said in a loud voice. "The best place ever," she said, more quietly, "was the clubhouse we made under my front porch with those leftover bricks and an orange crate."

"That wasn't half as good as the queen's throne room we made in the corner of my attic," I said.

"It was so hot up there we almost roasted to death!" Roberta yelled. She was mad. She went home.

I made a cozy place under the card table with
my quilt and a pillow. I took my notebook and my
colored pencils in with me. It didn't seem too
cozy. I drew a picture of Roberta getting mad.

Today after breakfast I went up to the back hill.
I piled branches to make a fort. I swept the ground
smooth and spread out my quilt. When I sat down,
it looked like a very cozy place. But it didn't feel
cozy.

I went outside to pick some flowers.   Maybe
that would help. Then I heard our secret whistle.
I whistled back. I saw Roberta through the trees.
She was coming up the hill carrying a basket.

When Roberta got to my new place, I invited her in. She sat down and looked all around. She took out two jelly sandwiches, two cans of root beer, some markers and a notebook.

"This is very cozy," said Roberta.

"That's just what I was thinking," I said.

THE END

Do you have a best friend,
or a cozy place?

(paste here)

Paste a picture here.